PARNIKA

SWARNIKA

To Pari,

As you bloom into a beautiful and wonderful being...

Contents

Acknowledgements

Working on this book has been a very personal journey for me as it commemorates the twenty-first birthday of my little sister, Parnika. She has been an essential part of my journey and I wanted to do something that came right from the heart. And what better way to do that for an introvert than using the mighty pen.

I want to thank all her friends for sharing the anecdotes on such short notice so that stories can be written based on these. Even I got to know about a few tales that I was unfamiliar with or had forgotten about. There were so many of these that we skimmed through them to come up with the ones mentioned in this collection.

I'd also like to thank Nishtha Trehan for helping me with this project. Your dedication to the skill is applaudable. I look forward to working with you more in the near future.

SWARNIKA

CHAPTER ONE

ICE CREAM CONE

Shruti's POV

featuring Shruti, Parnika, and Anushka

"We'll share the ice cream turn by turn," Anushka declares as we all pay her twenty rupees each.

We stand in the middle of the Mall road under the shade of a cone tree looking over us. The sun was hiding behind the mountain as the evening started to mend into the night.

We could see our class teacher gesturing at us to get back to the hotel in five minutes sharp. That should be enough time for us to finish our ice cream.

Anushka passes the cone for me to take a bite. The chocolate fills up my vision, tasting slightly bitter. My mouth freezes until I close my mouth and savour it, transforming it into sweetness.

With my eyes half-shut, I incline the cone towards Parnika to take a bite. She rubs her hands excitedly before taking such a huge bite that I'm left with just the cone.

Anushka and my mouths are open as wide as Parnika's with the exception that her mouth is full of mind-numbing ice cream.

"Oh, PP," I sigh as she tries to smile at us and fails.

Five minutes seem endless now.

We head back to the hotel after Anushka and I finish the cone. I get our attendance marked with the teacher and follow Anushka and Parnika to the room we're staying in. The hotel room had two walls, and there wasn't any window to see outside.

"PP, you should wash your hands. They're full of chocolate," I tell Parnika.

When she comes back, I try to hand her a towel, which she refuses before drenching me with water.

I gasp. "If anyone should be throwing water on anyone, it should be me!"

"Who's stopping you?" Anushka mumbles as she opens her water bottle and throws it at me.

"Oh, you didn't!" I squeal as I run to the washroom to grab a bucket full of water.

Ma'am is definitely going to punish us tomorrow. But that's not a problem for today.

CHAPTER TWO

FAREWELL

Parnika's POV

featuring Nandini and Parnika

Nandini and I move to the music filling the football field, crackling from a speaker bought from funds for farewell.

In a way, music flowed through us and between us, creating a stronger bond between us just like the day we danced in her PG.

We were giggling so hard after a girl knocked on our door and told us to tone it down. Spoiler alert; we just changed the song.

Nandini twirls and I leap to catch her arm as she falls, pulling me down with her. We're a puddle of laughter when she whispers, "Wanna take a break?"

"Yeah, as sure as we're on two legs and not crawling on four," I say and she gives me a big smile.

"How do you walk in a sari? I can't get up!!!" she whines as I pull her up.

"The trick is to wear heels."

"As if sari wasn't enough torture, I now have to hurt my feet?"

"The perils of being a woman," I sigh.

"The perils of being a woman," she repeats.

...

"Did I ever tell you I had a friend in school whose name was Nandini too?" I tell her as we walk out of college, bidding everyone goodbyes.

As she nods, I continue, "You remind me so much of her. I'm so happy that you're my closest friend in college!"

"Are you kidding? I'm the one who's grateful. You were the first person who was nice to me. You helped me settle, and that means a lot to me."

"Okay, we're both grateful," she says before I can argue. After a pause, she begins quietly, "I wish I could meet Nandini someday."

"Oh, you will! You aren't going anywhere!" I reassure her as I grab her wrist.

"I know right. Look at all those people crying." She points towards a group of people around the corner.

"They just don't have what we have."

"That's true." Nandini grins. "We are *school besties* after all."

I chuckle at that. "Good one."

CHAPTER THREE

No Cheating

Parnika's POV

featuring Nandini and Parnika

"Remember how you refused to help me cheat in college? Gosh, I wanted to hit you," Nandini continues as we walk forward, our college nowhere in sight. Is this how it felt when Nandu, Shruti, Anushka, and I left school?

A bittersweet feeling fills my mouth, and I have to silently count until three before I'm back in the present.

"That's because I have enough experience with Nandini."

"Oh, yes, the *school version* of me," she teases and I sternly shake my head. Nandu would kill her for this. She's the college version of Nandu in fact. But I don't say that out loud.

"Cheating is so tedious but it was soul-wrecking when Nandini was involved," I find myself telling her. "I'll do anything in my life except sit between her and Pratyush during exams."

God. I shiver at the memory.

"'Oh, PP, will you please ask Pratyush what the answer to c part of Q4 is?' 'Tsk, PP, ask Pratyush if $\sqrt{5}$ is the correct answer to the last question?' 'Parnika, tell Nandini to tell me the sequence of the MCQs' 'Parnika, tell Nandini that I am not sure-' Dear Lord!" I exclaim as Nandini bursts out into laughter.

"Parnika this, Parnika that, why don't you just shoot me in the head?!" I sigh loudly. "You won't believe me, Nandini, but one day I just told them to shut their damn mouths. I was oddly relieved."

She pats my shoulder. "That must've been hard. You are usually so calm."

"I know!" I tell her. "But you should've seen their faces. It was hilarious."

"Beware, dangerous Parnika ahead!" Nandini announces.

"Everyone should be scared of me," I say proudly.

"Everyone should."

But if I could go back and see the sight on their faces, I totally would.

I miss it.

CHAPTER FOUR

WATCH IT!

Nandini's POV

featuring Nandini and Parnika

"Cool watch!" I say as I glance at Parnika's digital watch.

"Thank you!"

"Did you steal it from Aniket?" I smirk as recognition crosses her face.

She grins in response.

"It was always fun to see you running around the corridor, wearing a watch that was bigger in size than you."

"Yeah, Aniket and I used to laugh about it," she giggles. "Nandini, you know what I think? I think he should have just gifted me his watch."

"Now that would've fun. A little larger-than-person watch order coming for Parnika!!!"

I click my tongue laughing before leaning across the table and grabbing her hand in mine.

"Let me try *your* watch," I say removing the strap from her wrist.

Before she can protest, I wear it on my wrist. I raise my arm, assessing it like it's a mystery that can't be solved, and then deadpans, "It's not huge on me."

"Maybe because you've grown," Parnika smirks.

"Or maybe it's because you're tiny."

She grab the pillow and throw it on my face as our laughter echoes in the room.

CHAPTER FIVE

FRIEND REQUEST

Shruti's POV

featuring Shruti, Nandini, Anushka, and Parnika

"You remember the time I used to dislike PP?" I bump my shoulder against Nandini as she shakes her head.

"Now, don't tease Parnika. You got to spend a lot of time with her, didn't you?" murmurs Nandini as she takes a sip of her latte.

I huff as I cross my arms and lean against the bench. It was me who decided to sit in front of the water fountain but I regret that as droplets of water sprinkle on my face.

"You're right," I say as Parnika's brow quivers. "I got to spend time with her and," I bring my face closer for dramatic effects, "it did not get better."

I laugh as it is Parnika's turn to scoff.

"Please, you love me."

"Who loves whom?" asks Anushka as she comes back from a walk in the playground.

"Shruti loves Parnika!"

"Shruti loves me!"

I roll my eyes as Parnika and Nandu speak at the same time.

"Oh, is that even a question?" Anushka looks on with consternation. "You both are inseparable. You're twin-flames, souls apart!"

Before I can open my mouth to protest, Anushka continues, "Do you guys remember that day in the playground in class sixth when Nandu had asked Parnika to join our grou-?"

"And how Shruti had said no instantly because she didn't like her?" Nandu adds excitedly, as if I could ever forget that day.

I was annoyed that out of all the friends Nandu could have, she had to be friends with Parnika. To me, Parnika seemed fine alone. Boy, how wrong I was.

"Well, I'm happy how far along we've come," I whisper to Parnika out of others' earshot. I've had enough teasing for one day.

"If that's code for I love you, then I love you too!" Parnika smiles gleefully.

Never going to live that down, am I?

I smile back.

CHAPTER SIX

10 CGPA

Anushka's POV

featuring Anushka, Nandini, and Parnika

A scroll of newspaper peaks out of my closet as I stuff the pile of clothes sitting on my chair.

"Cleaned my room, Mom!" I yell as I pull out the newspaper and gasp at the photograph of my girls posing as class toppers for the newspaper article.

A wave of nostalgia hits me as my mind flashes back to that time.

"We did it!" "We did it!" "We did it!" Nandu and I chant as everyone in the metro stares at us and thinks that we're a bunch of weirdos.

I couldn't care less what they think. My girls and I just topped school. How many groups can achieve that? None at all, I tell you. Except for mine! Hah!

"We topped school!" I mouth to a lady who constantly keeps staring at me.

She gives me a thumbs up and nods at me as if saying, "Oh, these girls make sense now" and then goes back to looking away.

"Okay, that's our stop," Nandini says and practically pulls me out of my seat because I am too high to touch the ground full of mere mortals.

"10 CGPA, isn't that super cool?" I excitedly yell before getting out of the metro.

"Great, now the people in the metro not only hate us but are also jealous of us," Nandini says as we head to the rendezvous.

"I know right. Hatred never felt so good." I grin at her.

An hour later when our group photograph is shot, I pull at Parnika's ponytail and tell her sincerely, "I'm so proud of you."

"Really?" her voice cracks before she clears her throat. "I mean, I'm proud of you, too."

"Yes, really." I pat her cheek. "And you're really brave, okay? You were brave enough to cry in school when you scored less in maths. You were brave enough to pull yourself up. I know how demotivating low marks can be and all the pressure that teachers put on us doesn't help. You're so brave and look at yourself... And before you say anything," I cut her off, "crying is brave. It means you care... you care about something enough to work hard towards it. That's brave."

"T-thank you." Parnika's eyes glisten as she wraps her arms around me.

I remove my own arms from around me as I snap a quick shot of the newspaper and send it to Parnika. As soon as the message is seen, I call her.

"Invite the girls over tonight for butterscotch ice cream?" we say at the same time and that's when I realize; she knows.

And that night we all unanimously agreed that the brick is too much for us to eat. And together, we finished it all in a few scoops.

Just like old times.

CHAPTER SEVEN

SEATBELT

Featuring Parnika, Pratyush, Shruti, Nandini, and Anushka

Pratyush burps, earning all of the girls' collective groan as they walk out of Mcdonald's. As they all head in the direction of the parking, Parnika hesitates.

"Guys, I have something to confess," Parnika mumbles, looking on distraught. Pratyush takes this moment to elbow Anushka and whisper something in her ear. That earns him a glare, effectively shutting him up.

"Um... I... I'd be happy if you all stepped closer for this. It's a bit difficult to say out loud," Parnika's voice quivers as Nandini, Pratyush, Shruti, and Anushka get concerned.

As everyone hurdles together, Parnika exclaims with joy, "Shotgun, suckers!"

"ARGH!" There's a collective groan just as Pratyush whines, "I told you, Anushka! I told you this was a ploy!"

As Anushka has the decency to look guilty and shrug, Parnika pats Pratyush's shoulder. "Get going, boy. You've got a seatbelt to strap on."

"Why don't you just do that from here? At least you'll be charged for murder then." Pratyush rolls his eyes.

"I heard that!" Parnika waves her fingers without looking back.

"Of course you did!"

"Seriously, what will you do without me?" Parnika says after everyone is in the car and she's in her favourite seat. Pratyush buckles his seat and Parnika connects the cable to the music system. Nobody has better music taste, after all.

"I'll be happy," Pratyush says, starting the car.

Parnika stays silent for a few seconds before saying, "But you'll be alive?"

"Isn't that a better gambit?" She smirks to herself.

"Why did you stop the car, Pratyush? We still have to go another lane before reaching Parnika's house," Anushka says nonchalantly from the backseat. Nandini and Shruti fell asleep while Pratyush and Parnika were busy bickering. Nandini stirs but does not wake up.

"For this," Pratyush answers with his hands intact on the steering wheel.

For a moment, nothing happens. Then Parnika takes deep audible breath before reluctantly buckling her seatbelt.

"This lane is the bane of my existence. Why do the Police have to roam around here?!" Parnika grunts.

"Maybe because there's a mall nearby?" Pratyush replies as he starts the car again.

"Ugh. I hate the mall too."

"No, you don't," Anushka says.

"No, I don't." A huff.

"Oh, you poor baby, did you have to put on seatbelt?" Nandini murmurs sleepily.

Parnika pouts sadly.

"Don't look at her. No one has any sympathy for you," Anushka teases her.

As soon as the Police is out of sight, Parnika unbuckled her seatbelt. She's only in the car for another minute before Pratyush is pulling into her driveway.

"You couldn't have waited another minute?!"

"Not really, no!"

"What would you do without me-? Bupp, bupp, bupp." Pratyush doesn't let Parnika speak. "You'll probably be in jail."

Parnika seems to ponder before saying and getting out of the car, "A convict is still better than being off dead."

"Hah, she got the last word again!" comes the cry from the backseat.

CHAPTER EIGHT

PILLOW STRETCH

Swara's POV

Featuring Swara, Parnika, and Rashika (Gul)

"That's mine!" I yell pointing at my pillow.

"Yeah! Yeah! She's a pillow-hog. If she could, she would have a hundred pillows on the bed and still wouldn't share." Parnika smirks.

"Hey! You need at least three to be comfortable. Ask a chiropractor, if you may." I shrug my shoulder quickly taking my pillows.

"Chiro who? Chiro what?" Gul looks confused.

"Chiro-doctor" Parnika tries to correct Gul.

I become the human embodiment of the facepalm emoticon listening to my little sisters sometimes and they do the eye roll really well.

"It's a chiropractor!"

"One and the same thing", Parnika exclaims.

"It certainly isn't", I sigh.

"Why did they complicate language so much? It's like they enjoy seeing others struggle.", Gul complains.

"You mean sadists?", I smirk.

"OKAY!!!! Topic Change. Topic Change. I'm bored with all this."

"Of course", I giggle. "Gul, you sleep in the middle."

"Okay di-", Gul is interrupted by Parnika.

"Anyway, I want my sweet corner." And there is that famous eye roll.

"Well, I want to protect myself from any late-night shenanigans you might pull in your sleep", I taunt her.

"What shenanigans? What does she do? Tell me. TELL ME!!!" Gul sounds impatient and I love telling this story.

"So basically, she loves to stretch in the Chakrasan pose... like the D sign-"

"It helps me be at ease!!!", Pari complains.

"Shh!!!..... So now she got quite used to stretch like that. We used to sleep right here in this room a decade ago. She started doing these stretches in her sleep. Imagine waking up in the middle of the night to see her elevated body. The first time I saw her like that I thought it was her body floating on thin air. I literally inhaled again when I saw her feet on the bed. I patted her head back to sleep."

"Wow!! Are you a witch? Are you haunted? This sounds scary. I hope you don't do this again. But I'll be fine knowing she's just stretching", Gull sighs.

"Yes, that was ALL that happened", Parnika tries to shush me.

"Wait, there is more? Oh god! What did you do?" Gul looks worried. I doubt she's going to get any sleep tonight.

"I... (giggle).... would tell you but you have to promise to sleep in the middle anyway."

There is a minute of silence. I continue after clapping my hands in excitement.

"So, we started sleeping in the other room after some time. Our bookshelves were there so it made more sense. One night she does her weird night stretch and after being startled for a minute I pat her head back to sleep. Suddenly she sits up. Her eyes are tightly shut and she's still asleep. She starts pointing in the dark corner of the room. Her hands are slightly trembling... She starts whispering, 'Don't go there. Don't go there. Somebody's other. Somebody is watching us.'...... There was no one. It was just a dark corner. I could feel chills. I literally froze. And this little girl, after scaring me like that, flips over and sleeps peacefully not remembering anything at all in the morning while I couldn't sleep all night. I was literally hiding under my blankie all night."

I feel the chills again.

"Di?"

"Yes?"

"Can you please sleep in the middle?"